Hunting for Fur

The Adventures of Panda and Koala

by **Thierry Dedieu**

DOUBLEDAY

A DOUBLEDAY BOOK

Bantam Doubleday Dell Publishing Group, Inc.
1540 Broadway
New York, New York 10036

First American Edition 1998

Originally published in France as <u>Chasse à la Fourrure</u>, © Éditions du Seuil, 1998
Doubleday and the portrayal of an anchor with a dolphin are
trademarks of Bantam Doubleday Dell Publishing Group, Inc.

Library of Congress Cataloging-in-Publication Data

Dedieu, Thierry.
[Chasse à la Fourrure. French] Hunting for fur :
the adventures of Panda and Koala / Thierry Dedieu. —1st American ed.
p.   cm.
Summary: When Panda and Koala agree to help a freezing wolf get
his fur back, they retrieve other stolen furs as well.
ISBN 0-385-32636-X
[1. Fur—Fiction. 2. Panda—Fiction. 3. Koala—Fiction.] I. Title.
PZ7.D35865Hu 1998
[E]—dc21   97-53077
CIP
AC

The text of this book is set in 18.5-point Italia Bold.
Manufactured in U.S.A.
October 1998
10 9 8 7 6 5 4 3 2 1

"Look, Panda! Do you see what I see?" said Koala. "Let's go warm up by the fire."

A wolf was sitting by the flames.

"Don't come any closer," he shouted. "I haven't got a hair left on my body. A bunch of thieves stole my fur, leaving me to die in this freezing weather."

"Not to worry, Big Bad Wolf," said
Koala. "We'll get the scoundrels. You
can count on us."

"That's right," said Panda. "Watch out, all you fur thieves! We may be small, but we're as strong as bulls!"

Panda and Koala headed
toward the big city. They quickly
put their plan into action.

"Shhh, not a sound, Panda,"
whispered Koala. "I hear someone
coming. Let's hide here."

Panda and Koala
took cover.

"Good thing we came prepared," said Panda. "Our old granny trap ought to work like a snap!"

"Freeze, you rabbit, mink, or wolf skin thief! That fur is ours!" yelled Koala as he and Panda jumped out of their hiding place.

Soon Panda and Koala had
collected a bundle of stolen furs.
  "Hey, push, Panda," puffed Koala.
  "Then pull!" said Panda. "That
sure was a good hunt. We really
made out."

Wolf was glad to see them again. "Thank you, my friends. Without you I would surely have died."

All that day, Panda and Koala
were very busy.
   "Next! Next one in line,"
they repeated in turn,
"please step up!"

"Panda," said Koala when they went back to town, "it looks like our cousins in Africa need a helping hand."